FREDERICK WARNE

Published by the Penguin Group
Registered office: 80 Strand, London, WC2R ORL
Penguin Young Readers Group, 345 Hudson Street, New York, N.Y. 10014, USA

First published 1917 by Frederick Warne
This edition with new reproductions of Beatrix Potter's book illustrations first published 2007
This edition copyright © Frederick Warne & Co. 2007
New reproductions of Beatrix Potter's book illustrations copyright © Frederick Warne & Co. 2002
Original copyright in text and illustrations © Frederick Warne & Co., 1917

Manufactured in China

APPLEY DAPPLY'S NURSERY RHYMES

BY BEATRIX POTTER

FREDERICK WARNE

APPLEY DAPPLY,
a little brown mouse,
Goes to the cupboard
in somebody's house.

IN somebody's cupboard
 there's everything nice,
Cake, cheese, jam, biscuits,
 — all charming for mice!

APPLEY DAPPLY
      has little sharp eyes,
And Appley Dapply
      is *so* fond of pies!

NOW who is this knocking
at Cotton-tail's door?
Tap tappit! Tap tappit!
She's heard it before?

AND when she peeps out
there is nobody there,
But a present of carrots
put down on the stair.

HARK! I hear it again!

    Tap, tap, tappit! Tap tappit!

Why — I really believe

    it's a little black rabbit!

O LD Mr. Pricklepin
    has never a cushion
        to stick his pins in,
His nose is black
    and his beard is gray,
And he lives in an ash stump
    over the way.

Y OU know the old woman
who lived in a shoe?
And had so many children
she didn't know what to do?

I think if she lived
  in a little shoe-house —
That little old woman
  was surely a mouse!

Diggory Diggory Delvet!
A little old man in black velvet;
He digs and he delves —
You can see for yourselves
The mounds dug by Diggory Delvet.

GRAVY and potatoes
In a good brown pot —
Put them in the oven,
And serve them very hot!

THere once was an amiable
guinea-pig,
Who brushed back his hair
like a periwig —

HE wore a sweet tie,
As blue as the sky —

AND his whiskers and buttons
were very big.